NORTH BEACH AND OTHER STORIES

a collection of flash fiction

Independently Published and Promoted
Socially Engaged Kink-Friendly LGBTQ Erotica
Cerebral Smut for Literate but Twisted Motherfuckers that
Give a Damn about the World and the People in It.

NORTH BEACH AND OTHER STORIES

a collection of flash fiction

by

PW Covington

Hercules Publishing

Albuquerque, New Mexico, USA

ISBN: 978-0-578-43765-1

North Beach

I sprang from the back of the car in front of the North Beach Hotel on Kearney, my legs unsteady.

I'd made it halfway across the country on five cocktails and two commercial airliners, landing at SFO about an hour after the early November sun had run off the edge of the continent.

The regal, worn, Asian woman at the counter had me sign what I needed to sign; "No smoking in the room", "No guests after 10", yeah, yeah.

She made a copy of my ID, a Texas drivers license with a dated phot of me; shaved head and a just-out-of-prison-long-enough to have grown the damned thing Fu Manchu mustache.

I got the code to the Wifi and took the elevator to

my room, 116…on the third floor.

The hallways were dark; old, but clean. Carpet in forest green checks, and dark, varnished, wood.

The place was a shit hole, but it hadn't gone to shit through dereliction or neglect. I knew that a lot of effort was being put into keeping this shit hole the kind of shit hole that it was.

Glorious North Beach shit hole. Perfect shit hole. Non- gentrified, proletariat, shit hole.

One of the last. Bodhisattva shit hole.
Hallowed be they name.

I unpacked my single case in a flurry. Enticing smells wafted up, to and through the opened, unscreened window in my room.

A mix of Chinese noodles, Korean BBQ, something sweet like doughy jelly…man, I was fucking starving!

I'd eaten at Gatti's pizza before leaving Austin and had hoped that would be enough to see me through until morning, but the drinks and the sudden energy of the vibe of the people of the street of The City got to me.

I needed to eat something.

There was a hunger that wouldn't be denied. Maybe there was a diner around.

Back down the elevator, out the front door, past the regal, worn, mistress of all things that needed signing, I turned right.

The noodle places, both of them, that I had taken not of whilst spinning out of the car earlier were closing up, so I kept walking until I came to a corner.

I never go into a place when they are closing. I try to respect everyone enough to give them a chance to knock off from work a minute or two early. Back to families, lovers, loyal dogs and hungry house cats.

The signs here were mostly bilingual, written in Chinese and English, some only in Chinese, but a noodle shop is a noodle shop no matter how it's written up, right? And every fucking one of them was closing up for the night.

The street climbed, uphill, and pulled me along, past neon red-kissed awning, Jackson Street daring me into Chinatown proper, but no…not tonight, not right now.

Food.

The smells of restaurants, all five minutes from closing, kept luring me, fueling my feet, my mind left out of it mostly.

This was pure Id.

An alley opened up and loomed on my right, just past

a place called Bund Shanghai…red paper lanterns hanging from a third or forth story balcony.

These two seconds, I knew, I'd remember forever in the heart of my mind's eye.

Yes.
Yes.
Loving it.

But, no to Chinatown.

Hungrier now, and walking faster…there has to be something still open.

Another right on Beckett, narrow, holy, Beckett Street, with its murals and clothes hanging out to dry on balconies. Neon buzz drifting on the cool, damp, air. And, that's where I headed…following the red and yellow glow up Pacific to Columbus. The pit of my stomach was growling.

A smoke shop, glass pipes and bongs in the window

before me, and I go into the deep space. There are glass counter tops and two men in the very back. I need some screens.

I brought my pipe along in my checked bag, and just enough stash not to be detected. But, the screen's been needing to be changed for a while, clogged with the resin of a hundred sleep-starved Texas nights.

The dark-eyed olive men look like brothers thin, stubbled beard-faced, and eager. All I need is some screens.

How many you want, the tallest brother asks.

How much do you charge? (Back in Texas, the shops sell them 10 for a dollar).

I can sell you a whole bunch for like 5 dollars, the guy says.

I don't need a whole bunch, I'd just lose them. Just

a few will do.

The shorter, darker, brother laughs. Yeah, I know
what you mean.

Tell you what, how many will this get me?

I fish 2 one dollar bills out from my pocket and lay
them on the counter.

The clerk puts 10 dime sized metal screens into one
of those tiny plastic bags that you only see in the drug
culture. This one has tiny pink mushrooms printed on
it.

I thank them both and leave the headshop grotto,
back out onto Columbus, right past Vesuvio. The ghost
of angry, bitter, fat, drunk, glorious, Kerouac taunts.
We have drunk together here before, on previous visits,
but won't tonight.

I walk past tourist couples from the Midwest, taking
photos in the alley. Digital cameras and cell phones.

No more negative images.

Everything is perfect, everything is instant, everything is existing as a mirror image and shared. Proof.

Proof that we were here.

Proof that we were there.

But, no proof of life. Close though, and some trips, close is good enough.

It's close enough for the workers at City Lights; glowing cathedral, fluorescent, bookstore. They are sweeping the floor and tending the shelves.

This is the heart so many times broken.

The hunger in my stomach, like the hunger of that sidewalk...Tosca taunts from across the street.

A busker with a massive white dog decide him on the sidewalk. Probably the real thing, probably a rail rider, a hitchhiker, a pilgrim…he's tuning a guitar, but never actually playing it. Looks sober, too sober for this night and a nod to him as I walk by.

The nod says, I've been there before, maybe I still am. Never give up on yourself, brother. You can fuck life in the ass all night long and still respect it in the morning.

Live, pilgrim, live…but I know that he knows all this.

Then, I find it.

At the right place at perfect cosmic time, serving by the slice.

I only need one. Pepperoni.

Nothing tastes like hot, street pizza. Texans never get this right.

The cat at the counter, ethnic, gives me a slice on a thin paper plate, and it is so hot that it burns my hand as I hold it.

I leave the shop and lean up against the wall outside, the corner of Broadway and Columbus, looking up the street at the gaudy, tantalizing, moving neon promising topless dancers and cocktails.

The Condor, Roaring 20's, Big Al's, and The Beat Museum; I'll be reading my poetry there tomorrow night.

It's enough for me to just stand here, the pepperoni of the Universe folded in my hands, orange-red grease staining the white paper plate. I stuff it into my mouth like a man who has a bus to catch and an alibi to conjure.

An older man, black, with his road-worn cotton beard stands next to me and asks me to buy his charity newspaper, and I just can't.

He understands and we talk. We talk about cheap food in Chinatown and strippers and cigarettes. He claims that he can get me a woman, but I know what he really wants is a quick $5 bill.

I change the subject to the weather, at least it's not raining as 10pm tourists flow by, all between bites of the best pizza, the sought after and found pizza, the beat pizza right next to City Lights, the neon born and West Coast pizza, street-style Italian,

About a million times better than Mr, Gatti's Austin. It's not just my stomach I am feeding.

Spanish.
Chinese.
German.

The word-sounds from passers-by tell me that this is international pizza, that mine is international hunger, that the man beside me is internationally beat. From this street corner, where MUNI buses and fire trucks turn, to the farthest, darkest, star; galactic hunger…it's all that anything's ever been, right here.

Not much more to it, really. Just that galactic beatness.

It still exists…even here, where it is packaged and sold; so, I finish the crust and fold the plate in half, then in half again, then in half again. Grease stained wedge.

I turn away from the cotton bearded man, who seems to be heading across Broadway somewhere, off towards the twin spires of Peter and Paul. I float back by the beautiful busker and his white dog, tossing the oily plate wedge into a street-side trash can.

Like the hotel, this street is seedy, worn; but clean, respected, maintained.

Beat is being down, but not out…never out…never out of the game, never out of chances, never out of hope, never out of style.

Back past the glass windows of City Lights…books on display holy Mexican santos. The sacred only works when it's approachable.

How many have sat upstairs with the poetry, not as shoppers, or even readers…but, jut to be and listen to the walls, the shelves, the roof top laundry drying just outside the open windows?

How many have rushed in, just to buy a Tshirt or bumper sticker, to take a Facebook photo or…?

Columbus runs at a diagonal, crossing both north-south and east-west streets, all the way through North Beach, and I follow it now, back onto Kearney, back towards the hotel.

There is a sink in my room, but I haven't a cup or glass to drink from, so I duck into a boba place and order a medium green tea with black pearl boba. The clerk makes it in front of me, as I drop my coin change and a dollar into the tip container. I grab the tea and a straw and walk back out to the street.

I'll drink it once I'm back in the room.

Into the lobby, past the regal woman who seems to be turning things over to a pudgy male clerk.

The elevator is full of twenty-something Korean tourists. Hip-hop ear-buds and hooded sweatshirts.

"3", I say, when one of the young women asks me, having switched to English for my benefit…the old white guy, probably down on his luck…probably lives in this shit hole…be kind to him, he's a big guy, but harmless, her dark eyes say as she presses the button and smiles.

The Morning Before Valentine's Day

I was sleeping as she woke, my deep, contented, breathing filled our chamber in a soft and comfortable rhythm.

Her sex was still liquid and warm from last night. I had been so excited to have had the rare chance to be inside her. I had been consumed with passion and urgency. I pushed myself not to disappoint, pounding hard into her from behind for almost thirty minutes after she had teased my poor, undeserving, cock to the point of free-flowing fluid three times over the preceding hour.

Of course she had denied my climax…in fact, I had cried and whimpered. I had begged her desperately, the final time, with tears of frustration and devotion flooding from my deep brown eyes, not to push me over the edge. I would never want to return to the way things were between us before; when we both foolishly thought that my orgasm was a normal…even desirable, part of our sex life.

I had used her body savagely last night, and she had fought back with even greater primal energy, as my bruised and skinned back, thighs, and ass testified.

The dried blood on our sheets, from her French manicured nails' attention greets me as my eyes open and focus. My scrotum burns in sharp, stinging, pain.

She had been an awesome fury to fuck. And, then, it was over.

After her final, last, climax, she drifted off into deep and satisfied sleep, knowing that my male member was left engorged and covered in her fragrant juices…satisfied that I would be left with that delicious, conflicted burning in the pit of my soul, crying out for more physical release, but content with the psychological denial and devotion that is the core of our eroticism.

She rolls over in the morning light and reaches for me. She finds my cock swollen, as it always is when I am next to her. I am warm, under the comforter, and my sore testicles are loose and pendulous, as she most prefers them; finely cut and recently scabbed over, just as she left them, hours before.

She cups the tender flesh in her soft palm and begins applying gentle pressure. My shaft responds. The throbbing intensifies. She brings her full, pink, bare, lips to my ear and blows warm, loving, morning breath softly upon me.

"Do you like that, baby?

"Do you like waking up with your balls in my hand, little boy?"

"Yes…", I murmur, still half-asleep.

"I know you do. I want to squeeze them this morning for a little bit. I want to hurt them for you before we get out of bed." And, she does. Slowly, she increases, then releases the pressure.

"Mmm…thank you, Sweetie…tha…thank you."

We've covered this all before. Every time she does this. Whenever she squeezes my testicles, I thank her, out loud. It doesn't matter how hard or how subtle she is with her attentions; no matter how adoring or cruel. We both love the surrender and control in this demonstration of our intentionally inequal physicality.

"You fucked me so good last night, babe.

"Thank you, that last orgasm was the best! I kept imagining that it was Ronny back there, taking my pussy, and that I was squeezing and ripping your little balls, hard, just like **THIS**, as he had his way with me." She squeezes me sharply and brings me into full consciousness.

She re-opens last night's wounds on my tender flesh.

"Thank you, Baby…", I take a breath inward, my cock harder now than it was, minutes ago in slumber. I know she can smell the sex on me from last night, carried on my body heat. She mentions it as she keeps pressure on my nuts.

"I don't want you to shower this morning. I want your cock and poor, little, balls to smell like me all day, today… You know, tomorrow is Valentine's Day…"

"Yes, it is, Babe. It's too bad that you have to work tomorrow night."

"Yeah, I'm sorry you had to cancel those reservations at Zinc down in Albuquerque, babe, but the double-time they are offering right now on the unit is just too good to pass up. It won't last forever.

"But… I've been thinking…"

"Yeah, Babe?"

She squeezes me again, hard.

"Thank you, Lover", my voice catches.

"I think I want you to find me a young, hard, cock for tonight, sweetie. Can you do that for me?"

"I'll try, my Love."

"Single guys always seem to be on the prowl around Valentine's Day; it shouldn't be too difficult to find a quality specimen. I don't want anyone coming here, though. Try to find someone staying at a hotel. Maybe around the Plaza area.

"You can take me over to him tonight, but I want to see a few choices first…faces and cocks.

"Do you understand, babe?"

"Of course, Beautiful. You deserve the best. Only the best, Baby."

"Good." She squeezes me again, even harder;

holding her grip this time as she leans over and looks at me directly and matter-of-factly, inches away from my face.

"I *really* needed to feel a man's hot load inside me last night, but we both know that we can't allow that from you. I need you to find a *real* man, with a *real* *cock*, to fuck me tonight.

"You know that's when I love you the most, right? When you bring me hot, new, cock and watch me get used like a slut?"

"Yes, Baby, thank you so much." My words are breathy. Tears are welling in the corners of my eyes. She is gripping me like a vise. "I love you so much, too."

"You're such a perv." She relaxes her grip and gives my circumcised and iron-hard, six and half inches a few solid tugs, "maybe. Just maybe, you can find a hot, young, bisexual guy.

"I'd enjoy watching you suck a nice cock tonight…think of it as a Valentine's treat. My present to you. But I want his first load in my pussy, okay?"

"Yes, Baby. Thank you so much. Oh, I love you. I'll try my very best.

"Clean, professional, **honest**, bisexual guys are pretty hard to find, even here in Santa Fe, but, I'll do my best."

She returns to her abuse of my balls, pinching and rubbing the skin of my sac.

"Yeah, I don't want us to drive too far, either, it's supposed to keep snowing all day…like I said, the Plaza area is fine, but out by the outlets, not so much. Maybe a couple around our age, but you know how picky I am." She laughs as she coaxes a trickle of red from my aching flesh.

"The things other couples talk about or secretly fantasize about, are the things we feel safe enough with each other to actually *do*. We really are rare, Peter.

"A cock-sucking submissive husband and a ball-crushing, chubby, 50 year old bitch that loves to be treated like a slut by younger, hotter, men with bigger cocks than she married." She giggles.

"The rest of humanity's got some catching up to do."

"Thanks, Lover. I'll do my best, and keep you posted."

"I know that you will." She gives me one last squeeze. "Thanks for the fucking last night. You really awakened something. I'd be nowhere near this turned on if you hadn't treated me so well last night.

"Seeing your cock ooze like that, then the way you pleaded with me not to let you come. You know that I love that. Baby, you actually cried. I get so fucking wet when you cry for me.

"And I loved destroying your poor, bloody, balls."

"Yes, Baby, I know. I'm very happy that you own my orgasms. My cock, my balls; everything. And that you feel safe enough to share all of your pleasures and fantasies with me…even those that you can only get from others.

"Thank you." As she squeezes me one last time, her palm now coated in my redness. She pecks me on the lips and rolls out of bed towards the single bathroom.

I am never allowed in there until she's finished in the morning. That was established the first morning after I moved in.

"I'll be out shopping with my trainer and his wife most of the day, but I'd like to see my options by 5 or so this afternoon…and, remember, I want you smelling like my pussy all day, babe.

"Change the sheets and take care of your balls.

"You can put some antiseptic cream on them and wrap them in some nonstick gauze if you think you need to, but that's it. I don't want you showering until I get fucked by another cock."

24 Hour XXX

The big city.

Well, not that big of a city; Austin, Texas.

The big city, that's where it's easy to sin. Easy to just slide around the corner and get that fix. Shit, you can do it on your lunch break, or on your way home from work. Blame the traffic if your wife asks. People that live in cities have it too damned easy. It doesn't take any real work to be a deviant.

When you live in a place like Terry lives, it takes a lot of work to be a sinner. It requires planning, no small amount of lying; it takes time and excuses and gasoline. It takes commitment to the cause, driving for an hour or more over secondary highways, getting stuck behind oilfield trucks, and negotiating 35 mile per hour, speed trap, towns. You can't just turn around if you start feeling shame or doubt…not after you've made all the excuses and told all of the lies. You don't dare carry a bottle along with you for courage because a speeding ticket is one thing, but a DWI arrest, towing, impound fee, all the rest…it'd be too damn much to explain.

No. If you're gonna do this, you need to be committed to carrying things out with mindfulness.

They are the kind of places that you never feel perfectly at ease going into.

Maybe you leave everything of value in the car, and only go inside with your ID and some cash. Maybe you take off your watch, if it's valuable enough. Terry always took off his wedding ring and stashed it in his pick-up's dashboard ashtray. It was part of his ritual. Maybe you carry a knife in with you, one of those little fold-over jobs that had the word "tactical" somewhere on the package it came in when you bought it. You've never been in a fucking knife fight in your life, but, still.

You've seen the places, sometimes just off a remote Interstate highway exit, sometimes in beige industrial parks…the really skuzzy places always seem to be next to no-name convenience stores that have signs advertising: "BEER-LOTTO-CIGARETTES".

It was the skuzzy ones that Terry liked best, like the one about a half a block behind Cavender's General Store off highway 183 in Austin.

24 Hour XXX, that was Terry's destination tonight, after midnight, as he came in from somewhere named nowhere, over 100 miles southeast of Austin.

"$3.00 minimum to enter arcade," read the sign over the hallway that led to the corridor of flimsy, plywood cells, each with their own pornographic DVD being shown. The game was; you bought tokens that you used to feed the machine in each little room, to keep the video going. Tokens were five for a dollar, and even though he'd been here enough to know better, Terry always bought $15.00 worth of tokens, out of a $20 bill.

That's a lot of little metal tokens.

The videos in the booths would show it all; muscle gay sex, trans stuff, MILFs, barely legal, even that fake assed plastic "lesbian" shit…just about anything except true scene stuff. Actual BDSM scared the types that came here. In each little room, there was a place to insert the tokens, but the videos just played anyway, whether you feed the kitty or not. Terry always deposited at least half of his tokens in the first booth he entered, anyway. Sin should cost a man something, right?

The spaces between the plywood booths were bathed in fluorescent light. Harsh, low rent, unending; it offered a poetic, if not entirely designed, harbinger of the evening's ultimate emptiness. Inside each, the booths were mercifully dark.

Every booth played a different DVD, straight ahead gay male ass-fucking was the offering in the first one when Terry opened the door and looked in. The booth was empty, and, as had been the case on his previous visits, the button that supposedly changed the selection did not work. The performers on the screen were attractive and muscular in a gym-honed way, and they were packing the kind of meat Terry had never seen in real life between their thighs, but basic gay porn was not Terry's thing. Terry was **not** gay. He tried another booth.

Two doors down he found a MILF-themed MMF three-way video playing, this would be better for him. Standing there in the middle of the small booth, ledge-like benches surrounded him. Some had torn cushions, their stuffing glowing in the television's reflected light. Terry's world narrowed to include only his lust. The woman on the screen was being plowed from behind while taking another hard cock in her mouth. Terry began stroking himself through his pants as he stiffened.

Two minutes later, the woman on the DVD, a tall, white woman with dark hair and a hint of sag above what remained of a very expensive breast enlargement surgery, was on her knees, taking the two men; one white and about 30 years old, the other black and in his early 20's, in either hand. Terry had unzipped his fly and had pulled himself out, openly stroking. There was no knock, nor was one expected, when another figure, shorter and softer than Terry, entered the booth.

Terry did not make eye contact but kept stroking, his eyes glued to the picture tube in front of him. The stranger reached out and touched him. Terry just growled, "Suck my cock, fag."

The man went to his knees.

A full hour later, Terry walked back out through the harshly lit retail area of the arcade where a token selection of DVD's and toys were displayed. He had held himself back, time after time, having been serviced by a total of five different men, all without ever making direct eye contact, all without speaking anything but the most basic of commands. "Suck this cock…" "Take it deeper…" "That's enough…"

It was the kind of place that you were always a bit nervous walking into, and it was a place you could never leave fast enough.

Before the final man, who took his pent-up load without spilling a drop, had even left the hot, humid booth, Terry had the keys to the truck in his hand.

The parking lots in these places were enigmas, there always seemed to be more vehicles outside than there were people inside, and the cars that filled them, after midnight on a weekday, weren't heaps, either. Classy sedans, late model pick-ups and SUV's, bumper stickers for Republican political candidates and "My Child…" window decals.

These were chimera places, places where men, and the occasional thrill-seeking couple came to let their "other" sides out for an hour or two.

No one was accountable. No one would ever answer for anything that went on in places like this.

This was a place where God wasn't watching. It had to be, because this could never be a reality, not for

Terry, not for any of the men that came here.

These places were not part of the real world, the world where they attended Church with pretty and socially stable wives, the world where they worked at respectable but repetitive jobs for decades, and harshly judged anyone that didn't exhibit the same strength of character they had shown all their lives.

The world that Terry sped back to now, out Highway 183, navigating the traffic lights that were now almost all flashing yellow, was his reality.

It had to be.

He always stopped at that one last 24-hour convenience store before the toll way to Lockhart began. He went in and selected a Dict Coke in a 16-ounce plastic bottle, his buzz needed to be gonc by the time he got home. Terry made small talk and exchanged pleasantries with the store clerk and a Travis County deputy sheriff at the counter. It would be a while before Terry would be back this way again.

It was a damn good thing, he thought, as he pulled back onto the highway, fishing for his ring in the never-used ashtray, that he didn't live closer to the city.

This city is full of faggots and degenerates.

It's just too fucking easy for them.

SGLI

$400,000. SGLI.

Servicemembers' Group Life Insurance

Fucking Robbie.

I hadn't even heard he had been killed until I got all
the paperwork, forwarded from that years old address
on the base in Kansas.

Shit.

He had died in Mosul, or somewhere like that. Some
kind of explosion. I found his name online in a list of
soldiers killed that month, but it didn't say exactly how
it happened.

Benefits awarded "By Law", the paperwork said. I guess we *were*, actually, technically, married…like, legally, now. Even in Texas. No one in his family even told me. His parents always hated me. Hated us. I hear that they buried him at that big Army cemetery in San Antonio. I heard it was free. I imagine there was a bugle and a flag. All that shit.

Fucking Robbie.

I didn't even have a checking account, and it took me over a week to find a bank willing to let me open one, just so I could deposit the check. I couldn't find any other way to cash it. I have the starter checks, brochures about mutual funds and Certificates of Deposit. The lady at the bank said that I need to "put my money to work for me".

Is it really my fucking money?

It still isn't real to me. How am I supposed to feel? I was on the phone begging for a couple of extra days to pay the light bill, while that money was doing whatever it takes to clear and post to my account. It took five days, there was a weekend involved.

I got cut back to like 15 hours a week at the dollar store, because it's the summer now and kids are out of school. They always hire three or four students. I put in for a job with the city a few months ago, but never heard back from them. I think I didn't do good enough on the typing test they made me take at the employment office over in Cuero.

What now? Does any of that even matter?

It's not like I have a shoe box of old love letters or photos or nothing.

A few emails, and my phone still has some pics on it. Pictures of his cock; pics of me sucking his cock. One picture of him, driving, on the beach at Port A, four days of growth on his face, but his hair is buzz-cut and military. In his last email, from when he was over there the first time, he accused me of fucking around on him with a Mexican guy that worked at the meat packing plant.

I was; and, there were others.

That was two years and three months ago, right after I had left him and moved back to Yoakum, goddamned, Texas. After that, nothing; not a text, not an email, nothing; until this.

It's not like he owed me nothing, and I sure as shit wasn't expecting anything from him. The last time we were together he left me with a fat lip and I almost stabbed the fucker. We were no good for each other.

Robbie was more the marriage kind than I was. We talked about it some, and did it in secret, in California, that time on vacation…I was never even for sure that he'd sent the papers in, officially. We didn't tell nobody but a few of our friends. Drinking buddies, really.

I guess I have some decisions to make. I guess I could go anywhere and start a new life. That sure sounds nice, but it's kinda overwhelming. I could buy almost any house I wanted in this shitty little town. But, do I want a house in this shitty little town? Where else would I live?

It's too much to think about.

The first thing I bought with my new debit card, the

one with a $399,000 balance, was a bottle of Bourbon, a Diet Coke, and a pack of cigarettes from the only liquor store in town. On the way home, I filled the tank up with gas. I never even watched the dollars and cents add up as they rolled by on the Exxon pump. That thousand dollars I had to put into the savings account, so I could get the credit union to open my checking up, is more than I've ever had in savings before in my life.

Maybe I'll get a new car. Maybe I'll drive over to Victoria tomorrow. That would be nice.

I guess I've got some decisions to make.

Fucking Robbie.

First Date

Lydia and I met through an online dating site.

We were both in our late 30's, and both new, again, to the area.

She had lived in Europe for over a decade, and had been married, until she wasn't, to a man she had met while working as a technical contractor on a NATO military base in Belgium, and I, against my better judgement, had recently accepted an offer from a community based mental health provider to manage a new group outreach program. We'd both grown up in the area, and as we chatted and messaged, it became apparent that we each felt distant and removed from the prevailing Conservative, "faith and family", social mores and values that permeated everything from dating to the job market, there.

She had moved back less than a year ago, and was staying at an unused, family home there. She'd just found a job with the local community college but was waiting for a few of her international credentials to clear before becoming fully "on-boarded" to faculty.

Our early conversations and photo exchanges were polite and respectful. For days, we learned more about each other's interests and habits, tastes and experiences, families and pets. She expressed herself well with words, used few emojis and avoided "text speak", which absolutely kept me interested.

I never pushed or pressured her to send me any pictures of herself, but when she did, I was not disappointed. She was dark haired, well over five and a half feet tall and curvy. I've never had a particular, physical, "type", but I did find her attractive.

Messages through the dating site were replaced by texts via our phones, then we shared social media information and Facebook profiles, as we opened our lives to each other. Pleasant conversation turned to flirty banter, and, eventually, she began pushing things into the erotic realm.

-"So, I noticed that you haven't sent me a photo of your penis yet? Are you not proud of it or something? LOL", she texted me late one evening.

I wasn't sure how she was expecting me to respond. Was this some kind of test? In our conversations, even as things turned flirty, I had always tried to allow her to set the pace; to allow her to remain fully comfortable with both the subject and the tone of our conversation. Whatever was meant to be, would be.

I decided that self-depreciating humor might be best, here.

-"Well, yeah, I DO like it just fine, thank you. But, it's no BIG deal, really. Lol", I texted back.

-"You'd be surprised. Some guys send pics of their twisted and contorted erections before they even send a picture of their face. Wait. You don't have any kind bend or deformity, do you?"

-"lol…Nope…Maybe mentally. That's all. As far as what's in my pants goes, it's pretty much straight forward and fully functional, lol"

-"Well, THAT'S good to know 😉", and she changed the subject.

-"You know, I enjoy texting with you a lot. You're respectful without coming across as insincere. I like that. You're a nice guy, but not a 'nice guy', you know, Paul?"

-"But of course m'Queen, lol… <3", I texted back.

-"Ohhh…'Queen', capital 'Q' and all. A gal could

get used to that, 😉 ", she replied.

We chatted a little more that evening before both of us had to get some sleep, but we agreed to meet up, the following evening for a meal at a chain casual dining restaurant, that, in our present circumstances, was, sadly, one of the most desirable places to meet for a meal in the city of just over 50,000.

-"I'll be out running some errands in the country all afternoon and might not have cell service, but, I'll meet you there at 8, paul. I'll be wearing black and red.", she ended our text session.

I didn't immediately think about it that night, but as I re-read our conversation the next day, I kept noticing that she hadn't capitalized the "P" in my name. Even after joking earlier about my capitalization of 'Q'...

It was exhilarating and exciting to me. I must have wanted to text her 10 times that day and ask her about it, but I didn't. This woman seemed like an amazing person, someone I could really become close with, and I didn't want to overplay anything or come across as a creep.

I got to the restaurant about 15 minutes early. There was no wait, and I asked the teenaged greeter for a corner booth, at the far front end of the place. I had worn a black T-shirt, tan slacks, and a blazer. I'd been on a few dates, with a few women, since moving back here and they had all shown up wearing jeans and had commented about how "dressed up" they thought I was…wearing a jacket. Most men here rarely took the time to dress themselves in anything beyond a logo'ed pull over, a ballcap, and denim.

Like I said. I didn't fit in.

I didn't particularly want to.

She arrived at exactly 8pm and immediately made eye contact as she approached and strode past the greeter.

Instead of attempting to conceal curves with black,

as many dresses designed for more voluptuous women attempt, hers seemed to accentuate her hips, her thighs, her bust, with red. The hemline cut mid-thigh and while the shoulder straps were wide, the neckline plunged in a very attention-grabbing way. She walked to the table with purpose and I rose to greet her. She offered me a hand.

"Well hello, Paul. You look nice."

"Please have a seat, Lydia, you are stunning!", I replied as she slid into her seat, her firm hold still on my hand. Her nails were tastefully manicured.

We looked at the wine list and she chose a bottle of Argentine red. I asked about her day and she told me about some relations of hers that lived in the next county over; cattle ranchers. She hadn't seen them since before leaving for Europe years ago. She spoke about growing up with cousins that had never left the area, and how she had uncles and aunts that only came into town for church or to buy groceries. It was a familiar story; one I knew only too well, but I loved watching and hearing her tell it.

Her eyes held mine like traps of hazel. She never demurred, never broke contact. Occasionally, I'd avert my glace to look around the room, to sneak a peek at her chest, to examine the menu or study the wine that glowed in the glasses before us. But, when I'd return, hers would be there, just as before, deeply and certainly focused on mine.

She'd sip her wine, and, as needed, I'd keep her glass refreshed

I'd nod, agree, every now and then, affirm something she'd say, but she seemed to be very comfortable carrying the conversation, so I settled in and just enjoyed being in the presence of this incredible person.

When the waiter came for our entrée orders, she asked me quickly if I liked spicy dishes. I said that I did. She suggested the chicken diavolo, even though it really didn't go with the wine. She ordered the petite filet, medium rare. I ordered the diavolo, and another bottle of the red. She smiled at me.

"You aren't trying to get me drunk, are you?", she asked in teasing tones.

"What? With your continental palate, I doubt I'd stand a chance. If you notice, I haven't exactly been keeping up here with the grape juice."

"Actually, I have noticed. A lot of guys down here would be on their third or fourth Bud Light by now. Do you drink beer, Paul?"

"No, not really…maybe one, at a party, to be social, but I'm more of a white wine kinda guy. That and maybe a Bourbon or Scotch at the end of the day."

"Hmm…", she purred. Her phone rang.

"Oh, this is a friend of mine, I have to take it. Excuse me."

I slid out of the booth as she stood up and headed toward the bar area, bringing her phone to her ear.

She hadn't returned when the waiter came and uncorked the second bottle of wine. I told him that I wanted to go ahead and give him my debit card, and that when we were finished with everything, whenever that might be, he could just go ahead and deliver the bill in full, already charged. I wanted to avoid all the awkwardness of the "I've got this", first date, money, BS.

It took a little explaining, but the kid finally understood…I guess (after I assured him that "my wife" would be right back).

As our entrees arrived, I watched Lydia return. This gave me another chance to admire the power in her stride. The sway of her hips and the confidence of her thighs, jutting forward with each step; her head high, shoulders back, her smiling at me as she owned the dining room was more intoxicating than anything Argentinean vintners had ever bottled and sent away to these shores.

I half rose as she reclaimed her seat across from me.

" I don't want to sound presumptuous, Paul," she looked at me in mock conspiracy, "but, do you think you could give me a ride home after dinner?"

"The wine hitting you that hard? I'm sure we can re-cork this bottle…", I began to say

"Oh, not at all, actually", she grinned as she lifted her newly filled glass. "No, it's just that I'm going to let my friend, the one that called, use my car for a little bit tonight…I told them you'd be able to get me home. They're gonna swing by in a few and pick up the keys. You don't mind, do you?"

"No, I suppose not."

"Awesome. It's not far; my place is super easy to get to, it's just across the highway from that big, new, high school. This looks *DELICIOUS*!" She cut into her filet.

"So…", she looked from her plate, a few minutes later, lowering her glass from her lips, "I want to thank you for an absolutely enchanting evening, Paul. You really know how to show a girl a good time."

"Thank you, Lydia", I replied. Her eyes captured mine.

"No, I really mean it. It's like real respect…I mean, I know that you're trying your best to impress me. We're on a date, and we both want things to go well, but there's something about you. I can tell. Something about the way you're treating me. Maybe it's the way you treat all women?"

"I don't know, exactly. I like to think I treat women the way I'd like to be treated…pretty much the way I'd hope to treat anyone else," I said.

"Maybe that's it", she held her glass out for me to fill. I reached for the bottle and poured again.

"Of course, you *are* hoping to feel the wet folds of my recently repatriated American vagina around your cock later tonight, aren't you?" It was all I could do not to spill the fucking wine glass in my hand. She giggled "Yeah, that's not gonna happen, Paul…not tonight"

"You just had to see how I'd react, huh?," I shot back, mildly, once I'd recovered enough composure to verbalize again.

"Yeah.

"And, you did alright. I'm sorry, sweetie." She reached across the table and caressed my arm, giggling.

We finished our meal in much higher spirits, the wine and her bawdy ice-breaker helped keep the conversation animated. When the waiter asked about desert, we shared a slice of mediocre cheesecake. Lydia was impressed when the bill arrived, along with my card, needing only a signature.

"Preparation is the key to success, wouldn't you agree, my queen?" I teased, as I slid the Visa debit back into my wallet.

"Indeed, squire…indeed," she winked. "Speaking of such manners. Let me text my friend. Do you mind if we move to the bar for a few minutes and wait?"

"Of course not, I would enjoy a Bourbon, anyways"

"Okay, then, I'm going to visit the ladies' room. I'll meet you at the bar?"

Lydia hugged me and pressed her warm cheek against mine.

I started a new tab at the bar, ordered a double Makers on the rocks and selected a dimly lit table along one side of the small room.

Lydia returned from the ladies' room with fresh makeup. By the looks of things, she had touched up her hair as well. She slid her chair close to mine and joined me at the table, against the wall, facing the bar. As we both sat down, her shoulder and upper arm lingered against mine. The feel of her body against mine was warm and electric.

She leaned over and whispered into my ear seductively, "I think I've had more than enough wine tonight, but I'd love a night cap cocktail."

"Then, please...by all means...", I gestured at the bar, "There's a tab started."

When the waitress came, she ordered a Long Island Iced Tea. She turned back to me leaning in, again, to my face in a way that invaded my space in a very welcome way.

"I'm sorry about coming across so forward, earlier. I guess I tend to forget myself when I've had a glasses. I just want you to know how comfortable and safe you make me feel, Paul. You're a perfect gentleman. I really feel like I can just be myself around you." Her eyes had locked onto mine, again.

"I think that's one of the most sincere compliments a woman can pay a man, Lydia. Thank you."

"No, thank you", she winked back and broke eye contact, as the waitress brought her drink in a tall glass.

"A toast!", she raised her glass, and her voice, "To new things in old places!" I lifted my tumbler and touched her glass. We each took polite, moderate, sips.

Her phone dinged, "…Oh, there he is now. My friend, Tommy. Let me text him and let him know where we are, he can join us for a quick drink", she invited him into the bar area of the restaurant.

About two minutes later a very large man, dark

skinned, well over six feet, and hefty; 300 pounds if we were in Texas at all, came in, and Lydia's eyes lit up. She jumped to her feet and ran to him, arms out.

"Tommy! You old scamp! Still up to your dirty tricks I see, let me feel you!" She embraced him, curling into his bear-like frame, pressing her face deep into his chest, then looking up into his eyes before breaking the embrace.

I rose from the table and offered him my hand.

"This is Paul, the guy I've been telling you about, " she introduced me.

I hadn't known that I'd been discussed. He shook my hand with a firm, meaty grasp, and then sat down next to Lydia, who had moved to sit across the table from where she had been seated, with me, before Tommy had arrived.

"You MUST have a beer with us!

"Paul, would you be a sweetie and order Tommy a Bud Light, please…just a long neck, I don't want him getting a DWI and having the cops impound my car, now!" and she motioned to the bar with her eyes.

As I moved that direction I heard him reply in a deep baritone,   "Well, it wouldn't be the first time, would it, sugar tits?", then, giggles.

I asked the bartender for the Budweiser Light longneck, on my tab, and brought it back to the table, where Lydia and Tommy were laughing.

It was obvious that at some point they had been lovers, maybe more, and that a friendship remained, maybe more. They were getting along very well and to be honest I felt pangs of jealousy swelling somewhere within me even though I wasn't sure I had any right to be experiencing them…or relishing them quite the way I was. Lydia seemed to be evaluating and diagnosing me with her eyes, almost as if…no.

But, maybe. Just play it cool and see, I told myself.

I handed Tommy the cold bottle as I sat down across from them. He took it and smiled at me.

"So, Paul, you must be packing some serious meat

to have attracted this one's interest. You know, she used to have quite the reputation as a size queen, around these parts."

I cut a glance over at Lydia, who was feigning shock and coquettish discomfort with his directness. My reaction was anything but feigned. Before I had a chance to react, she spoke, batting her eyes at Tommy, then resting them on mine.

"Which is Tommy's *very* sophisticated and subtle way of letting you know that we have been lovers…and that he *does have* a huge cock," she giggled.

Tommy was smiling as he took a long pull from the dark bottle. "Which you always handled like God's gift to dick," he teased as he sat the beer back on the table across from me. "I've still got those pictures you wanted us to take."

"Ah," Lydia winked at him and leaned in against him, "the better to remember me by, stud."

Just play along, I kept telling myself, this could get interesting.

I was trying my best to present as the well-groomed, heteronormative, 35-ish, guy on a first date; completely uninterested in the wonders and diversity of all things penis, but, like anyone willing to be honest with themselves, woman or man, I can absolutely appreciate a well formed, well presented, larger than average male organ, and were you to examine my Pornhub history, the search term "BBC" may make an appearance or five.

"Then, a toast, to Tommy's massive cock, and all the women that have taken it!", I raised my glass to chuckles and laughter, all around. Across from me, the two made eye contact again and clinked drinks, then he reached across the table to me. Lydia was studying my face again…but for what exactly?

Did either of us know, exactly?

Lydia spoke up.

"Which kinda presents the question, Tommy…I assume that you'll be using my car this evening to meet up with one of your would-be conquests. What's up with your truck?", she asked him.

"My wife is using it tonight, supposedly helping a friend of hers move"

Oh. I see, I thought to myself. I just sat there, smiling at them, my mind whirling and my pants secretly shrinking in the crotch.

"Man, this conquest was won long ago. This one is just a full-out cock slut. I'm picking her up after work and taking her to that adult arcade out across the county line. She lost a bet last week that I couldn't or wouldn't fuck her until she passed the fuck out from cumming," Tommy laughed again… "so, tonight, she's gonna suck every cock that gets put in front of her face. While I pound that pussy, of course…Hey, the whole idea was her idea, her fantasy. You know how the bad girls love me, Lydia"

"Sounds like a lot of fun, you dirty old man!", again, she slapped him lightly on his bulky upper arm.

Tommy looked at his watch and replied, "Which, actually…I do need to get going, she's almost off work and I want to use every second she's got tonight, along with every hole." The big man laughed and started to rise. "Thanks for the beer, Paul. And thanks for everything, Lydia."

"No worries, Tommy…have fun tonight…maybe I'll text ya later, if you're not too buried in pussy."
"Play it by ear, girl," he concluded, standing and finishing his beer. He walked out of the place with her keys in his hand and her eyes followed him, through the front window, into the parking lot.

"I'd love to apologize for him, Paul, but…THAT'S my friend Tommy. We really were quite the item back in the day." She was giggling, but, in no way shamed.

"Hey", I said, "as long as I get to see the pictures sometime," in good natured perversity.

"That," she replied, "might be an opportunity that requires earning. My ex-husband sure enjoyed them, though; and the videos, too" She brought the last sip of her drink up to her lips. The ice cubes clinked in the glass.

"Hey sailor, let's get out of here. Why don't ya give a girl a ride home?"

I let the comment about her home movies pass without comment. "I thought that you'd never ask, dear."

I got up and went to the bar to close the tab.

The bartender, a pretty, Latina, college student, was beaming at me, bright eyes and glowing smile. "Y'all seem like really great friends, Mister Cavanaugh. Did you three go to school together or something?"

She'd looked at my card for my name…and had obviously overheard at least some of what we'd been saying.

"Actually, I'm the new guy on the block," I laughed as I signed the slip. "He's a friendly ex of the woman I'm here with tonight."

"Your friends sound pretty cool," the young woman said, then wished me a great evening. I'd tipped her $10 on the bill.

Lydia was getting up from the table when I returned. "I'm impressed with the way you handled that," she told me as she moved close and allowed me to wrap an arm around her. "I was hoping you wouldn't be embarrassed or anything. Tommy can be a bit much for some guys."

"And probably some women, too," I raised an eyebrow and looked down into her eyes with an impish gleam.

She tilted her neck up and kissed me on the lips, right there at the tableside. We left the restaurant holding hands.

Sitting beside me in the car, she took my hand and placed it on her thigh as we drove, the GPS unit directing us to her place. It seemed as though every traffic light was destined to be red for us this evening. At the second one, she told me, point blank, "I want to feel your hand on my cunt, Paul". She slid forward in the seat and the hem of her dress slid up. I ran my hand up her thigh, my eyes never leaving the road.

"You didn't wear panties tonight," I observed.

"I did. But I took them off, earlier, when I was in the ladies' room.

"Preparation, success, and all that…now, show me what you've got, Paul," she brought her right foot up and placed it on the Ford's dashboard as the light we had stopped at turned green.

By the time we pulled into her driveway and stopped with the engine running, in front of her closed garage doors, she had brought herself to two climaxes grinding against my hand.

It doesn't seem fair to take much credit for "making her come". Her need was an undeniable force riding with us.

Her clitoris swelled so full and hard, at times it felt almost like I was stroking a small cock, and she encouraged me in open, blatant, obscenities to get her where she needed to be taken. It was so erotic and so powerful. This was a woman that would not be denied until she was fully satiated.

I put the transmission into park. She grabbed my hand and leaned over, taking my fingers deep into her mouth, into her throat, slightly gagging herself; pure lust in her eyes, as she locked them onto mine. Her left hand found the crotch of my pants and squeezed…hard.

I had been swollen since we left the restaurant.

This woman had been full of intoxicating surprises this evening, and that continued when she pulled her head from my fingers and moved to kiss me hard and deep, forcing her tongue past mine, into my mouth. She asserted her will upon me as the truck idled, there, outside her home.

"Take your cock out for me, Paul", she told me "I'm going to suck you, right here", she told me.

And, that's what she did.

My God, her lips and tongue felt heavenly!
It was too much to take. It was embarrassing how quickly she pushed me over the edge.

After weeks of online teasing and after such a stimulating night in this very smart, very sexy woman's company, despite the interruption from that brutish friend of hers…*fuck…why am I even thinking of him while this goddess has my hard member in her amazing mouth?*…I just couldn't for the life of me, hold back. But I didn't want to NOT feel her delicious mouth on me, either.

At the last moment I let her know, "Oh, Lydia…Oh, Lydia, You're making me come!"

She brought her head up just slightly, moving me from the back of her throat into her mouth. I blasted jet after jet of hot semen into her. It felt like a solid minute, one after another, I went light in the head. She pressed the tip of her tongue against that spot underneath the base of my cock-head as I came…*shit*!

I must have given her every drop I had.

When my spasms had finally ended, she pulled off of me and brought her arm up, to the back of my neck and pulled herself up…she leveraged my face close to hers and kissed me again.

This time, she filled my mouth with the seed she

had just drawn from me, feeding and forcing it back to me with her strong tongue and soft throat. Purposefully, passionately, she rubbed my neck and ran her nails through my hair. Her lips sealed themselves as she pulled away and looked into my eyes.

"I'd really like to see you on a regular basis, Paul, but, I do have certain expectations of the men I allow to share my life…you were just introduced to one of them. When I let you orgasm, you will swallow what you ejaculate. Can you agree to that for me?"

Her eyes were locked on mine. There was neither humor nor malice revealed in them. It was something…else.

I really didn't know what to say.

Of course I had tasted and swallowed my own semen before, but she didn't know that…or, more accurately, I didn't know that she knew that.

The salty taste of my fluid, along with just a hint of her residual sex was intoxicating as it mixed with the aroma inside the pick-up's cab.

One of her well-groomed eyebrows arched in the streetlamp and dashboard glow.

"Look, dear. I had a wonderful night, but things are going to be certain ways…if they are going to be, at all…between you and me. You're a sweet guy, Paul, and I like sweet guys. In fact, I think you'd be pleasantly surprised at how much I know about how much I know about the things that you need from a woman like me, Paul."

She moved her hand to my face and caressed my cheek as she spoke softly; my cock slowly going soft in her other warm hand.

"Paul, did you have an enjoyable evening with me, tonight?" she asked.

"I hope you know that I did, Lydia", I whispered.

"Yes, I know", she said. "You need to know that nothing that happened tonight was an accident or a coincidence, though. I'm very glad that you can appreciate the value of preparation, Paul.

"You see, Paul…I had certain suspicions, certain feelings about you…and, I wanted to see how correct I was about them before going any farther with you.

"My wine and menu selection, Tommy's 'unexpected' visit, our little play on the ride home (you'd be surprised how many guys have no idea at all how to find the 'little man in the boat')", she giggled, "and, I have to say, lover, you've left me very impressed.

"But, I want you to go home tonight and think.

"If you want to be in my life, on my terms, for as long and as much as I want and need you, on my terms, and for my benefit, then I'd love to welcome you, to cherish you, to love you…but, just understand Paul, it will always be on my terms.

"I do not expect or want an answer from you tonight.

"I want you to leave here tonight and think. I want you to think about how you really feel and about what you really need, and then, sometime tomorrow or the next day, I want you to invite me to lunch. Not dinner, lunch…at the restaurant of a nice hotel and tell me what you have decided. Can you do that?" Her gaze was direct and kind, but neutral.

"Of course, Lydia…and, I did have a wonderful time. Thank you for your company tonight." Damn, this woman was beautiful.

"Call me, Paul." She opened the door and got out of the truck. She walked around the side of her home towards her back door as she fished her phone and keys out of her purse.

For the next five years we were very content, very

fulfilled, very empowered; on her terms. We traveled the world and we grew, eventually growing beyond even each other. When we parted, we knew our years together had shown us things about each other and ourselves that we never could or would have seen with any other or in any other way.

It all started with that first date.

Day Sleeper

The sun comes up in the morning and safety returns.

The sun comes up in the morning and I get up from the keyboard. I open the drawer that is second from the top, on the right side of my desk. I take out my nine-millimeter, model 92F Beretta semiautomatic pistol and I carry it with me while turning off the air conditioners in the front part of the house. The pistol is identical to the one I carried two decades ago, and that I used in combat, on two different continents. The house is a wood-framed rental, built in 1912, in what was a booming rail-road town on the coastal plains of Texas.

I head back to my bedroom, and off to sleep. My dog follows me back to the room. He knows that the watch is over.

I strip out of my blue jeans, the same pair of pants I have worn two or three days in a row now and decide that they are probably good to go for another couple at least, and so I do not throw them too far from the bedside. The ceiling fan in the bedroom is on its highest setting. I can't remember a time when it wasn't spinning; turning like the hands of a high-speed stopwatch, only in reverse. The shades are cheap plastic miniblinds, yellow and brittle from the sun. They have been down and closed since I moved in to this place almost four years ago. I'm not even sure how to open them. The windows are sealed, closed with layers and decades of off-white, rent-house paint. Maybe it's just a matter of perspective, but this will be the coolest it gets all day.

The fan will stay on, as will the overhead light. I do not keep a lamp in my bedroom. The overhead light stays on until the light bulb burns out, and then I replace it.

I slide into the full-size bed and slip the pistol under my pillow. I have grown accustomed to its bulge and padded firmness against my cheek as I drift to sleep. It makes me feel...hell, I don't know how it makes me feel, but it simply reminds me of certain things, certain people.

My dog; an overfed, tan and white English bulldog, stands a bit back from the far side of the bed like he does every morning at this and he watches me. He knows my habits. He knows my routines. He knows my secrets, or at least I like to think that he does, and he seems to tolerate all of it better than any woman or wife I've had as a bedmate. When I am settled on my side, and after I have wrapped the Olive Drab linen keffiyeh around my head several times, blocking the light, both solar and electric, from glowing through my eyelids, the dog will jump into bed from the far side.

He knows that this is the routine, that this is what we do. The sun comes up and we retreat, withdrawal, retire. We leave the universe to the ones that do not know much about the realm of night creatures. We hand the world over, once again, to the multitudes that take the light for granted. Sometimes his rhythmic, guttural, snoring begins before I expire. When it does, it helps me to fall asleep quickly, like the cadence of the surf upon a gentle beach or the singing of crickets on a temperate summer evening.

Most of my days pass dreamlessly. Deep, satisfying sleep is a gift. Sleep is a reward for the living, and rewards can be especially enjoyable when they come with the suspicion that they have not been entirely earned through honest effort. Horatio Algier be damned, I enjoy deviant, daytime sleep. Most of the time.

The dog will stretch his entire body out on the bed, his head towards the foot, and more than once in our slumber, he will wake me up when he presses against me. I do not like to be touched, not while sleeping, not while awake, not anytime, really.

More than one wife or lover took it as an insult when I refused to indulge their mindless caresses or reacted with a violent startle after a surprise kiss from behind. The dog barely notices when I shove him away. I feel for my weapon and it is safe there, under my pillow. Sometimes, I just like the feel of it. Something about this touch soothes me.

Most of the time, I fall back to sleep quickly and enjoy several more dreamless hours.

Most of the time.

Round Top

I was all about the sirens' songs.
The sirens' calls,
Until the sirens called.

    I used to love spending time with desperate and lost
women…filling nights and weekends with bottles of
sweet and stinging liquors.

Women; young or older.
Women that would help me empty my wallet of
whatever cash I could scrape together.

    Then they'd tell me that they could borrow a couple
hundred bucks from a cousin…always a cousin.
They'd ask me to drive them some place. Then they'd
tell me that I'd have to split for a while; that they'd call

me when they had the cash, and that we'd hook back up then, once they had it.

I actually believed that shit, too, the first few times…

Sleeping in my car a few blocks from the Albuquerque bus station for a week, waiting for a call on a pre-paid Walgreens Tracphone, waiting on word from some red-haired chick whose mother was working in some program for recovering addicts bussing tables for the guys at the air base.

I guess she must have ended up getting clean and going to work with her out there, too, or something, without telling me about it.

Eventually I'd get the hint and take off to Nogales.

Arizona is a shit place, but I couldn't hang around that scene forever, just waiting.

You can go on that way a while, man…like an orphaned Maine-Coon kitten with a Roman candle up its ass, let loose down the aisle of a crowded

Mississippi church bus.

You can go longer than you'd ever give yourself credit for, anyway.

Fucking decades.

Then, it happens one day.

You catch your reflection in a mirror.

Maybe, in a motel somewhere.

Maybe in a bar, if you still hang around such dives.

Maybe, just in passing.

Probably, in a goddamned motel somewhere.

You're fucking 45.

Maybe, a year or two more than that, but if it hasn't hit you by 50, it probably never will and either you're a total shit-bird or a Holy Fucking Roman Saint.

Some kind of cock-sucking Buddha God-incarnate.

Fucking Kerouac never told you what happens now, did he?

Maybe he did. Maybe you need to go back and read *Big Sur* again.

One thing is for sure, you just don't have it in you to weep over any dead mice or dead dogs or dead birds or dead fish or dead whores or dead whatever the fuck it was he was always weeping about in his drunkenness.

Weep over one grand, dead, beat-up and cast-out world.

But you ain't got no tears for any of that right now. And this ain't coastal California.

This is Texas.

You've got three marriages, two wars, three felonies, a disabling psychiatric diagnosis, and more decisions made wrong than right behind you.

For better or worse you're a writer. You've done everything from drive trucks to tend zoo, but as things turned out, you're a writer.

You're a writer.
A poet.

I'm a writer and I fucking hate being around writers.

I mean I have some writer friends but they are friends first.
They happen to write.

Some of them, most of them, maybe, might not even call themselves "writers" if you asked what they did for a living in the daytime.
Fuck them for that.

But, they are.
Poets.
Writers.
And, friends.

I have friends that I became friends with because we met as writers... but, I know few that I became friends with BECAUSE they were writers, if that makes any sense.

I read. I read a lot. I even read stuff that I hate. I read pure shit. I'll read shit just to try to figure out, why…exactly, I think it's so shitty.

Hell, there are terrible, young, reporters writing for my local paper that I read for no other reason. A select few are jewels among the shit, but most are shit among all the other slightly less shitty shit.

To actually spend time with most of the assholes? Fuck no.

I'm hiding from them right now. Yep. Hiding.

I'm shifting tone, shifting tense, shifting voice, bouncing between poetry
and prose, code-switching between the bar-ditches, fucking over all perspective, destroying dimension with desolation. Fuck it. It's what I do. Hiding; right here on the page

First of all, I'm at a fucking writer's conference.

Round Top, Texas…a pseudo-village of 90 people. It is spring time; the cultivated wild flowers are blooming, and everything is postcard perfect. Antique stores and rustic crafts line rural blacktop roads for exactly four miles in all directions.

Very Texan.
Very.
Former Governor Rick Perry occasionally spends long weekends with his family here.

I am renting a motel room at the cheapest place in the oilfield town of Giddings, 15 miles away.
Hiding from Governor Perry.

Hiding from the poets.

I checked in for the conference, got my registration packet and anthology, got my name tag, and got my tickets to the catered meals for the weekend; I got everything Round Top, Texas, figures I warrant...I got every damned thing I paid for, anyway.

I was taken aback when I discovered that the editors of the anthology had placed my piece on the page facing a poem by Robert Hass, the festival headliner, who had been US Poet Laureate for two years, back in the mid 1990's.

Shit, not THAT big of a deal, really, I suppose… his last year as Poet Laureate of the USA was the year I was arrested on my first felony charges.

Time fucks with all of us, don't she, Jack Kerouac? *I'm talking to fat, drunk, bitter, Florida, Jack here…but young, bright eyed, Lowell, Jack would do well to eavesdrop a bit…yes, he would…*

I mean, really?

"Who the fuck am I, to be here," I thought, as I looked around the manicured parking lot.

I've got a little over 120 or so college credit hours

Shit, maybe more than that, if you count the stuff from the Air Force Community College. In everything from Criminal Justice to Business Management, but I could never stick with one thing or stay in one place long enough to make any of it count towards anything. Then, by the time the war, and prison, and the streets, and living out of a bottle, or a pipe, or a bus station sink, caught up with me, my nerves just couldn't take a classroom anymore…I tried…I even tried online classes, once things started settling down for me.

It wasn't that I couldn't work or do the work; it was that it couldn't work for me by that point.

I spend a lot of time on college campuses and around professors these days; but, really, who the fuck am I?

I don't even have an Associate's degree to call my own.

HOW

IN

THE

FUCK,

MAN?

I wasn't in the mood to make new friends, so, I picked up what I had to pick up, exchanged my greetings, my hello's, my thank you's, my pleasantries, my brief introductions, FUCK, I suck more at this every year…and I got the hell back out of there.

Stopped at Wal-Mart on my way into Giddings and grabbed a bottle of wine and a frozen veggie personal pizza to take back to what both Hotels.com and the East Asian immigrant desk clerk assured me was America's *Best* Motor-Inn. Fuck the catered meals and the tickets. My room has a mini fridge and a microwave, so…veggie pizza and white wine works for me…only a few months ago, it would have been a bottle of Bourbon and a burger, but hey, remember that fucking mirror?

Good enough for a plastic motel cup and a toast to the imposter before me tonight.

Tomorrow there will be readings.
There will be more that I will want to hear than I will want to say.
And that will be perfect.
As it should be.
It will be time to gather.
Not time to cast.

I am still lured by sirens' songs.
Even when I know their every note to be futility and mirage.
A time to sit and listen to learned, respected elders.
Those that stayed in school.
Those that colored inside the lines.
To nod as if I give an appreciative shit,

For, perhaps I will,

A little bit,

At Round Top.

Dash T

It could have been six hours; it could have been twelve, since I woke up. My head rested on a table, my feet chained to a chair. I'd had nothing to eat since my capture… how many days ago? I'd pissed myself and the wet, canvas, pants were chilling me.

The door opened, and the lights dimmed.

"I'm Agent Sarah Rodriguez," the tall woman introduced herself, and entered the chamber, "I'll be administering your restoration treatment, then you'll be released". She brought a metallic instrument up from her side.

"Your full name and citizenship identification code." It was a demand, not a question.

"Stephanie Rose Jackson…two nine six, eleven zero,

eighteen forty four.

"Dash 'T'."

"Dash T's haven't existed since before you were born, Stephan. Stephan Ryan Jackson," the agent said. "You know that."

It came back, along with fear.

The raid, the gas, the way they beat Brandon with their plasma truncheons.

The fear returned, but the tears did not… if this was happening, I wasn't giving them the satisfaction of seeing my terror.

She brought the instrument to my scalp. "This is going to burn."

I woke up, on the ground, behind a brick building; dressed in the dress I had worn to meet Brandon. It had been cleaned, and I had my hair back.

"I love you so much, Steph." Brandon was coming to help me. "I was worried you wouldn't get the same Agent I did."

"Whaa?," I asked. All that really mattered was that we were here, together. Now, I cried.

"Rodriguez. She's one of us. She's with the resistance. And, she edited your C-ID data. No more looking over your shoulder, babe." He was beaming, even with a bruised face.

"Now it's time for them to look over theirs," I resolved.

"Chainsaw Gator"

It was midmorning and I had just returned to the dormitory. I had spent the last few hours at the prison infirmary undergoing a series of mandatory, pre-release, medical tests. Because of the high-risk nature of life inside Texas prisons, state law requires that all prisoners be tested for HIV, Hepatitis, and Tuberculosis before being released. A compulsory blood sample is also drawn for inclusion in a state-run DNA data base used by law enforcement to match evidence left at crime scenes. Ideally, this data base could also be used to exonerate those falsely accused or convicted of crimes as well, but the state makes no mention of that in the paperwork an inmate is forced to sign, before their blood is taken.

As the time remaining on my sentence shifts from weeks to days, I've been feeling a bit more disconnected than usual. The faces and names around me have changed so many times in my stay here that I have lost track. In my 58-man holding tank, I have now been here longer than any other prisoner. I have, though, seen two men released, only to end up back here again, with new felony convictions. For the past year, the arrival of new inmates has been a twice weekly event as county jails from across South Texas transfer in those sentenced to prison sentences of two years or less. With a dorm full of new faces, I live as I have since I got here, enjoying my daily routine of meditation, study, and correspondence. After a while all the stories and excuses begin to sound the same. I have been spending more and more time planning and contemplating projects that await me upon my release, and by doing so I have cocooned myself mentally from the continuing drone of convict events.

It is rare these days that I take more than passing interest in any of these new arrivals, so, when I returned to the tank from my morning at medical, I didn't pay much mind when, before I could even get to my bunk, a young Aryan affiliated guy came by,

"Check out that new white dude in bunk 11."

I got my white, plastic, commissary mug from my bunk area and added hot water from the restroom sink to a spoonful of instant commissary coffee crystals. I sat down at one of the stainless-steel dayroom tables and waited for the call for lunch that would come over the intercom speakers in an hour and a half.

My attention was soon drawn to a young man, maybe 21 years old, with his legs crossed on the state issue blue, plastic mattress, rapidly rocking himself back and forth. His hands were clasped in front of him. This was the "new guy" in bunk number eleven. As I kept a discrete eye on him, the frantic rocking continued. Others were also watching, snickering and pointing in knots of three or four, from different spots around the bunk-lined prison pod. They were watching but were also staying well clear of the area surrounding his bed.

It isn't unusual for those just getting to a new bunk assignment to keep to themselves or to feel a bit anxious, but this guy seemed really fucked up.

I walked over to the bottom bunk and the rocking young man, and in as pleasant of a tone as I could muster, spoke with him.

"Hey there. You just get here this morning? My name is Hugo," I extended my hand in greeting.

He took my hand and stopped rocking. His handshake was limp and heavy, it felt like I was carrying, instead of shaking, his hand. His eyes were tense and sharp. They darted quickly across my face and around the dormitory.

"Yeah....", his voice cracked, "Yeah, I'm not supposed to be...be here. I...I...want to go back to Bartlett. I...I...ain't supposed to be here."

Bartlett State Jail is a State Prison facility similar in scope to this one but designated to primarily house inmates from Austin and Central Texas.

"What's your name, man?", I asked.

"Ch...Chain...Chainsaw Gator. My name is Chainsaw Gator."

"Well", I said. My time in prison (and on the streets of Berkeley, California) has taught me not to express shock or dismay at things that might, at first, seem absurd. "Chainsaw Gator is kind of a long name. Is there something else I can call you?"

I try my best to avoid using the street or gang nicknames that many prisoners use to refer to themselves. Avoiding these often hyper-macho and usually dissociative alternate identities has often allowed me to relate with others in a more human, more fundamental way that the shallow interactions of street or underclass nicety.

"You can call me three things; Chainsaw Gator, Gator, or Chainsaw."

"Okay, well, you don't look much like an alligator to me, but I guess I'll call you Gator. So, they sent you here from Bartlett, huh?"

"No…No…I came in from Crisis Management at Sky View Unit."

Sky View is a lock up facility that convicts deemed as mentally or emotionally unstable are transferred to in order to receive psychiatric attention not generally available at individual prison units (of which Texas has well over 100). Usually, a prisoner must be an immediate danger to themselves or others to be sent to Sky View as a "Crisis Management" case. Because of a supposed lack of funding and a cost-cutting policy of "adaptive integration", stays at such correctional crisis centers is generally limited to a 60-90 day stay.

Fast, cheap, and on the fly interventions often get applied to circumstances where years of therapeutic and medicinal management would be ideal. At the end of this crisis management period, prisoners are sent back to facilities and into conditions identical to those that triggered the incidents or behavior that led to their removal. Trying to treat mental illness within the Texas prison system is like trying to put out fires with jet fuel.

With the slashing of public funds supporting mental health treatment and intervention, prisons and jails have become the only option for many with chronic mental illnesses and chemical dependency.

Bizarre, antisocial, and at times psychotic behavior are common parts of prison life. In place of expensive and time-consuming counseling or psychotherapy, prison and medical administrators most often resort to high doses of psychoactive and tranquilizing drugs to keep mentally disturbed prisoners sedate and compliant. This approach raises its own concerns about informed consent and over-reliance on pharmaceutical "quick fixes". But it does allow for the smooth, arguably safe, and disruption free daily operation of prison units, where many inmates are diagnosable as seriously mentally ill.

"They…they…they…sent me here. I'm supposed to go back to Bartlett. I don't want to be here. What can I do to get back there?", the young man asked me, his pointed eyes pleading.

"I don't really know. Why did they send you to Sky View? Can you talk about that with me? Did they think you were going to hurt yourself?" (Inside prison, it is a major faux pas to directly ask questions like "What did you do?", or "What is your crime?"…you always…ALWAYS frame the question as "What did 'THEY' *say* you did?"….lives have been taken because new inmates did not understand this).

"No…I…I…was in fear of my life there at Bartlett. They tried to…t….kill me there. They wanted to cut me with a knife."

"Well, if you were in danger at Bartlett, they probably won't be sending you back there, Gator. They probably sent you here because down here at Dominguez, we are in a different region. Why did the people at Bartlett want to hurt you?"

"Because….cause….I pissed in the air vent. Th…the…whole dorm was breathing my piss-smell."

"Yeah, Gator, I can see how some people would be upset about something like that."

In the code that convicts live by behind prison walls, personal hygiene is very important. Inmates that, for whatever reason, fail to keep themselves or their area clean and neat are deemed to be showing disrespect to those they are housed with. More than once, I've seen prisoners assaulted or threatened for not showering regularly or not keeping their bunk areas tidy. The behavior that young Mr. Gator, (Mr. Saw?), had just described IS the kind of thing that could get a person killed in any institutional setting, all the more so in a dormitory setting where "personal space", for the most part, simply does not exist.

"Why did you do that? You couldn't get to the urinal in time?"

"N…no…I pissed in the vent. I made the whole dorm smell my pee," Chainsaw Gator dismissed my attempt at an explanation with a malicious pride in his still darting eyes.

"Is that why they sent you to Sky View? Did you get any help while you were there?"

The young man looked confused. "Th…they have cake at the chow hall there."

While it is not uncommon for newly arrived prisoners to try to malinger and fake symptoms of mental illness in attempts to be left alone by others or to avoid unpleasant work assignments, I was quickly realizing that this young, red-haired and under-fed, fellow convict was probably dealing with some serious shit….shit that wasn't going to properly addressed in this dorm nor on this Unit.

"Okay, Gator. I'll leave you alone now. I just wanted to introduce myself. If you need anything, just let me know. I live just down the row from you in 8 bunk, okay?"

"Okay." He stared off again into the dayroom area and resumed his agitated rocking which had completely stopped while we were speaking.

By the end of the following day, many of the other men in the tank had begun teasing and making fun of Gator. He would remain sitting in his bunk for hours, never once altering or slowing the rhythm of his rapid, back and forth movement. As I mentioned before, this kind of stuff is nothing new to anyone that has ever had to spend any time at all living inside a prison. While unusual and attention grabbing, this perpetual rocking was already starting to become just another absurd "thing" here. Prisoners avoided Chainsaw Gator, and it was generally assumed that that was exactly how he liked it.

The next morning, I was sitting again at one of the industrial, steel tables in the dayroom, when Gator stopped his rocking and came to sit next to me. He started by asking if I could help him fill out one of the I-60 forms that prisoners are required to submit whenever we have an official request or question to ask of a prison official. He told me that he didn't feel safe in the dormitory and wanted me to help him write the mental health department and ask for a consultation. I helped him do so, but as it was a Friday, I tried to impress upon him that he would have to be patient, that no one would get the I-60 until after the weekend had passed.

He started rattling off a litany of frantic questions:

"Did I think this dorm was a safe place?"

"Did I know if anyone here wanted to kill him?"

"Did I think they would ship him back to Bartlett?"

"Did I think they would give him drugs to calm down and help him sleep?"

"Did I think this dorm was a safe place?"

I stayed calm and patient with him, as he literally worried himself sick. I explained that as long as he pretty much minded his own business and stayed clear of any gang activity, most likely, he'd remain safe and unfucked with. As far as his questions about assignment or medicine, I was honest and told him that I really couldn't say one way or the other. I told him how he and I were in the same boat, both prisoners, both wearing the same white, state issued clothing. So many of the decisions that affect our daily lives are simply not ours to make. I think that maybe it is learning to accept that fact, without resentment or despair is the secret to being able to come through an incarceration without it damaging your soul. Prison is an excellent place to learn the value of detachment.

I shared with Gator my own mental health history; how I have been diagnosed and treated for both Major Depressive Disorder (MDD) and Post Traumatic Stress Disorder (PTSD). I offered him my support and again stressed the importance of patience when trying to access help from the prison mental health system. As the young man with me at the table began to calm down, I could see the weariness that all the fear and anxiousness had etched across an otherwise child-like face. Before he even realized that he might have been enjoying a moment without desperation, though, he again tensed up and completely out of context, blurted out:

"Sometimes, I like to shit in duffel bags!"

"What?" Not exactly coffee klatch conversation. I was surprised and didn't do an extremely good job of concealing it. His volume rose and an element of what sounded like glee entered his voice as he continued. By now maybe a dozen other inmates were paying very close attention to Chainsaw Gator.

"Y....yeah, I shit in one of my friend's duffel bags- I threw it on his roof and now he doesn't like me anymore."

"Was this before you came to jail?" I gently coaxed, hoping to bring him back to the present reality.

"Yeah, but one time I shit on the floor of my Mom's house, too. I like to shit and piss in bags."

"But, you wouldn't do anything like that here, would you?" Other prisoners were openly laughing yet were taking careful note of every word Gator said.

"Y...yeah...at Bartlett, I pissed in the air vent- the whole dorm breathed my piss," the same look of satisfaction and malicious glee appeared that had been there the day before, but this time, he continued.

"An…and then at Sky View, I took a bag and I shit in it. I put it in my cellie's locker, the one under his bed. He said he wanted to kill me. I was in fear for my life."

From somewhere across the dayroom: "I'll fuck that guero up if he shits on any of my stuff!", followed by laughter.

"Look, Gator," I spoke calmly, still being friendly, "It'd probably be best if you didn't go around telling people stuff like that. They might think that you want to do something like that here, and that wouldn't be cool, okay?"

"No…no…I mean it. I like to shit in bags, sometimes in the sink, too," he was escalating.

"You shit in a sink around here, white boy, I'll kill you myself, you crazy fuck!" This time, the response was fired directly back at him from one of the more connected Latino gang members playing cards at a nearby table.

"Yeah, dude," I told Gator. "People don't like to hear that kind of shit, man." In a statement that seems utterly bizarre looking back on it, but that made perfect prison sense at the time, I continued. "Around here, we shit mainly in the toilets, Gator- sometimes, some of us do it a little in our pants- but, mainly, we shit in toilets. You willing to help us out with that while you're here, Gator?"

"Y…yeah, but just don't make me mad, okay?"

"Hey, I'm trying to be your friend here, man. I don't want to see anything bad happen to you. Just try to stay patient, whatever problems you're dealing with, we will see if we can find the right person to help as soon as we can, okay?"

"Yea…yeah…thanks. I'm just cra…crazy, that's all."

"Hell, man, we're all crazy in here. We're all just trying to get through this shit the best way that we can, okay? You ever feel like talking, you come and find me, man. Especially if you feel like you want to do anything that should be done in a commode."

I meant what I was saying to Gator, but I was also saying it to help calm everyone; me, Gator, the twenty or so black, white, and Latino gang members that had gathered around the table.

Chainsaw Gator was now as frantic as he had been the day before and faced the angering crowd. They split as he scooted back to his bed, where he started again with the rocking, quick metered and constant. He didn't leave his bunk for chow when it was called. It would be mid-afternoon before he stopped, having finally exhausted himself to the point of slumber.

It occurred to me a bit later that evening that I really had no reason to be nursing feelings of distance or separation in these final days of my imprisonment.

If I was feeling disconnected, it was a choice that I was making, a chosen denial of the reality that surrounded me. The universe is always there, all day, every day. I had, once again, started to believe there was an "outside" and an "in here". When I allow walls like that to start being built in my thinking, I am choosing to dwell in ignorance of the interconnectedness of all in each present moment.

Yes, I would soon be making a transition from one physical and emotional environment to another – just the latest of many transitions that life and greater existence holds for each of us. But what, I thought, about the ones that somehow get lost along the way?

There were days, there were moments during my sentence when it felt like the burden of imprisonment was going to pull me under. In these times of confusion, I drew inspiration from my study of Buddhist Dharma. I learned all I could about the awakened mind that is elemental and foundational in all sentient existence. If I ever can help others realize this level of peace and acceptance, healing and education, I decided that I wanted to do so.

I never saw or heard from Chainsaw Gator again after that week. A night after our conversation, he was moved, while most of the men in the dorm, including myself, were sleeping.

Prison is like that. Sometimes, people simply disappear with only memories behind them, memories, which in most cases, also fade and vanish quickly. In prison, as in war, the lost are quickly pushed off to the side.

Maybe they are recalled years or decades later. Usually, they are not.

10-54 Code Three

Flight delay after flight delay because of weather in Denver and some kind of chemical spill on the runway in Los Angeles. A tight, twenty-minute connection to catch the last flight out of Phoenix at 11pm on a Sunday. A credit card snafu at the parking garage in Houston.

Coming back home after two weeks out on the road never holds the kind of unbridled joy that they try to sell on sentimental family television dramas, but THIS TIME, before I could get in my front door, I had to deal with a fucking dead body on my porch.

An actual, dead, motherfucking, old man on my front porch.

I didn't touch anything. I took my bags back to my

pickup, sat inside, and called the cops.

"Hell, no, I don't know what happened. All I know is that there is an old dead guy on my front porch. Please, come and get him. Did I call the wrong place to handle that?

"Yes, I'm pretty fucking sure. He's stiff as a board…old fucker, too. No, I don't think I've ever seen him before."

"Stay where you are, sir, we have a unit on the way."

"Well, I can't even get in the door, the way things are right now, so I'll be out here waiting."

"Do you have a weapon, sir?"

"No, I have a dead guy on my fucking porch…

The police showed up, three cars, lights, sirens, the

whole show (have I mentioned that it was like 2 in the morning?). I was being yelled at, guns pointed at me. An excited, buzzed-cut, uniformed, 20-something ordered me to lay on the ground in my front yard, then handcuffed me.

Fuck me for finding a body on my porch, fuck whoever the ancient asshole was that chose to die there.

It was after six before an older, woman, officer came and opened the door to the backseat I was being held in "for your safety and ours, sir". She let me out, and uncuffed me.

They'd taken the body away an hour or so before, and, of course, the fuckers had been traipsing in and out of my house all night. The judge that came out to declare the dead man dead, had also shown me the warrant he signed allowing the police access to my home. I didn't want to have to fix the door yet, before getting some sleep, so, I let them use my keys to open the door. One of them had reached in taken them out of my jacket pocket.

I would have called my lawyer, if I actually HAD a fucking lawyer, and if I hadn't been handcuffed in the back of a goddamned patrol car. One of the cops had taken my phone as well "for safekeeping".

"Turns out the old guy had Alzheimer's and had a habit of wandering off, lived with his daughter up around the block….looks like he had a stroke," she said…."and," she continued, "the funny thing; he used to own this house and live in it back when it was first built. He sold it to the couple you bought it from, we checked that out, so…It doesn't look like you had anything to do with it. His daughter said that she was pretty sure y'all never met." She handed me my cell phone back.

"Yeah, that's what I told the dispatcher when I called you pricks"

"You're that writer, right?, " she asked me with a knowing smirk...."The one that hates cops, right?"

"Yes, that's me."

"How long were you in prison?" she asked, pointedly.

"Almost four years total, back in the '90s, counting county time for all the shit that was dropped or dismissed."

A crowd of blue was gathering.

The worst part of finding a dead man on my porch was turning out to be answering the questions that were coming now.

"So, what IS it that you find so disrespectful about police officers, sir?"

What the fuck kind of grammar was that? What did she even just ask me? Fuck it, never mind.

Three men had joined her now, and they surrounded me, my back up against the car from which I'd just been released.

Cop hands rested on cop belts as the sun came up. Five cars still surrounded the house; city cops, and one from the Sheriff's Department. Their lights had been on since they arrived.

My neighbors were getting quite a show before Monday morning work commutes. I could almost hear them rehearsing for the inevitable local TV news stand-up…" Well, he was gone a lot, and sometimes his grass would go two months without being mowed, I think he was a veteran or something…I guess he snapped. I don't think he actually worked anywhere…"

I was tired and beat, and needed to piss, so, what the fuck, I thought, I answered her question.

"No matter what, your job is law *enforcement*. Even, this, here, was really just a case of housekeeping. There was a dead motherfucker on my porch, and I needed him hauled off, so I could get in my house and enjoy some sleep, but for the last 4 or 5 hours, every cop in the county has been out here trying like hell to find some law to **enforce**.

"That's what you call yourselves these days. You're not 'peace officers' anymore (until one of you gets shot or run over or something), no, you're '*law enforcement officers*'. Shit, they don't even call them 'jails' anymore, they are 'law enforcement centers', am I right?

"Enforcement, enforcement, enforcement...that's the extent of it for you people.

"Not discernment, criticism, commentary...not even

improvement. Ever heard of a 'Law
IMPROVEMENT Agency' or 'Law
IMPROVEMENT Officer'?

"My issue with you folks and what you do, is that the
very BEST, the most professional, most honored, men
and women in your profession are *NOT* those
pioneering new thought or finding new solutions to fix
the things that we ALL know suck about society.

"No, the most respected among you are those that are
just the *best* at *not questioning* what they are expected
to do. A law gets broken and it's your job to enforce
law, right? It's a total fucking binary in your world,
isn't it?

"You know what? A lot of laws just fucking **suck**
and should no more be obeyed or listened to than the
words of a fairy-tale king or carnival huckster.

"Personally, the thing I respect most in any sentient
being is fucking *sentience*. To even KNOW that you
exist, you have to be free to respond and engage with
the people and the world around you, unrestrained by

fixed boundaries and limitations. We must ALL be free to make choices, free from coercion or threat, or by others' ideas or expectations about morality, legislated or otherwise. You guys actively oppose true independence…*with guns and the threat of violence.*

"A person that blindly 'follows the law' is far less evolved or interesting than one that understands the true reasons WHY certain things just aren't fucking cool to do. That wisdom only comes to those willing and able to freely explore the limit and breaking point of laws and social taboos.

"We don't need 'law enforcers'. We need citizens that have been allowed to actually LIVE and have come to understand *WHY certain ways are best*, not just being told that they have to do things a certain way or get they'll be thrown in prison.

"Law enforcement gets in the way of sentient, informed, personal morality. I do not like you because **you lack imagination** and moral courage."

Not a word from any of them. Shit, two of them wouldn't even make eye contact with me. Suddenly, the tops of their black, ballistic nylon, assault boots seemed very interesting.

"I had three hours of shitty sleep in a crappy motel, two nights ago, and I need to piss so bad, that you're lucky you aren't cleaning up the backseat of this car, right now.
So, unless you want to stand around and bullshit all day, can I have my fucking keys back, please?"

One of the younger, male officers, handed me my keys.

"Look, sir, we all have a job to do, okay?, " he said.

"Yeah, I guess we do," I answered and walked towards my door.

Onion Rings

The giant order of onion rings sat untouched.
Cheddar soup, half eaten. After midnight. Jim's Diner
on Fredericksburg Road, just south of the medical
center.

Kaylee, her 4 year old daughter, slept in the booth
beside her.

Christmas would mean a bus ticket. Another second
chance; another fresh start.

She promised me that this year would be different.
It was going to be her year.

She'd never see him again. Earlier today was the
last time. She swore it.

But, couldn't I lend her a quarter ounce of kine bud? Just until she got to Utah. She was going to quit smoking, and the pills too, when she got to Utah. She had friends up there that went to church, she said. Just until she got to Utah, just to get through December.

For old time's sake, she asked.

I just looked at the bill on the table. I asked for more coffee. I watched her deep, used, eyes and let her lies drift past me like plumes of smoke hidden by pre-dawn bile. I stared at the onion rings; crusty and cold.

Hark the angels.

Hark the King.

Hark, hark, hark.

Hark the herald onion rings.

She rattled on. She always knew I was a decent guy, and about the quarter ounce, and how she was giving it all up for New Years. The child snored in that way only the very young and the guilty can; no matter where slumber finds them.

Only until she got to Salt Lake. Only until New Year's Day. Crayons were scattered on the table. Her Houston Texans jacket with the dirty sleeves.

"Meet me at the Jim's by the medical center", her text had said. "Kaylee and I are leaving town. For good this time."
For good.

I just sat.

I watched her talk.

My phone buzzed. Again.

I sipped the coffee. It tasted like shit.

Her eyes were worn, like basins full of memories too heavy to carry around. There was a time when I thought she was more than a whore and a junky and a manipulative little cunt. Not that long ago, really. I watched her talk about Salt Lake City and I watched the onion rings. It might have looked like I was listening, but…

She was leaving Christmas Day, she said.

With Kaylee, she said.

And, about that quarter ounce…

You stay here, I finally said, and I slipped a $20 bill on the table. I'll be back for the change, and I'll bring you that quarter of kine. I stood up.

I blocked her number from my phone as I walked out of the diner. Then, I drove away.

She was leaving Christmas Day.
Again.

I was running late.

I was supposed to hook up with a couple of dancers around three at this crippled guy's place, across town, off East Houston Street. They needed to connect and had always paid cash, with no bullshit.

They'd texted me three times in the last half hour.

Damian

"You scared me a little bit, earlier, when you led the group into that bar…"

"The one off Avenida Reina?"

"Si"

"Hell, I needed to pee. Turned out that a couple of the others did, too."

"Oh, no big problem, and it was nice to have a few drinks once I was able to find you all, but it wasn't on the itinerary. Neither was that little place you all decided to eat lunch. I'm glad I caught up to you all," Damian's eyes shifted a little, from his beer to my face.

"The cafe was Olivia's idea. I wasn't even all that hungry. Hey, thanks for playing along yesterday when I brought you up on stage to interpret at that studio…you're a natural on stage."

"You write well. I enjoyed reading your work."

Damian reminded me a lot of a retired journalist I knew years ago in a little place in Mexico called Estación Creel.

Esteban.

Esteban had been a newspaper reporter in Tijuana for almost 30 years before he came to that canyon town in the wilds of Chihuahua. I found the way his skin crinkled around the corners of his eyes, and the way his silver-streaked hair contrasted with a seemingly perpetual youthfulness and smolder, very attractive.

We worked together, serving drinks, then, once we

found a trustworthy supplier, selling eighth ounce lids of weed to backpackers, at a place called Margarita's. I was hiding from Texas cops, and Esteban just seemed to be waiting. We'd shut down the bar and walk back to the row of adobe apartments where we both rented rooms. Sometimes he'd invite me over, and we'd drink, smoke, and sniff up a few lines. Sometimes he'd ask me to massage his back or to read, out loud, from an English translation of Pablo Neruda's poetry; other times it was Grateful Dead cassette tapes.

Most nights, I'd take him in my mouth before returning to my little garret. We kept things loose. Easy, unrushed, like the town itself, that sat at the midpoint of the Ferrocarril Chihuahua al Pacífico. That summer was a season between other seasons…there was no real pressure to hurry or end anything.

I ended up back in Santa Fe by the end of 1999, then drifted back out to the Bay Area, before finally getting sent back to Texas and that 2 year prison term.

I'm not really sure what happened to Esteban, but I saw something in Damien that brought him back, after all these years.

"Never mind. But, I did have to report in at my agency and let them know we had been there," he said, reaching out for the green, glass, Cristal beer bottle in front of him.

"Well, you know poets; we never have been much good at walking straight lines."

Damian nodded. His English comprehension was exceptional, refined. I suspected he had spent some time in the States at some point, but according to him, he had traveled some, but had always lived in La Habana.

"I do not know much about poets, but I do know that you left the American Air Force… how was it? Non-judicial punishment?"

"Touché, Damian. You've done your homework." I brought my glass to my lips and sat back in the padded, wooden, chair. "Yeah," I said, "Then, you also know all about the first unit I was with too, before it was dissolved. You know about Africa."

"Maybe... I didn't read that in your application."

"Maybe because it wasn't IN the festival application," I needled. "Neither was anything about that fucking Article 15, two and a half decades ago." Our eyes met and I caught something. I noticed a smile in those wrinkled corners of his eyes. I held his glance with slight and amused inquisition. We searched each other, silently, like co-conspirators, until the waitress interrupted.

"Si, señorita un otro, por favor, pero...tienes anejo?"

"Si, Havana Club anejo. Ocho años."

"Perfecto, un anejo mojito; y un cerveza Cristal por me mi manejador, también"

His lips parted as he nodded to the waitress. It was after 6pm, and just a hint of beard shadowed Damian's face. There was still plenty of natural light. It was early July, and what stubble was emerging, cast a silver sheen. We were at the bar at the Hotel Nacional, having drinks, while waiting on the owner of tonight's paladar to call from Old Havana and say he was ready for us, the delegation of US poets.

He looked out the large, glass windows; the ocean was choppy. High, grey, clouds, turning slightly orange, stretched to the horizon. A dark-haired woman, maybe 35 years old, lounged poolside in a turquoise bikini. "Manejador! Por favor, I am just a guide…here to make sure you enjoy yourself in La Habana."

"How many years were in prison, Patrick?" Damian asked, directly, when our eyes met again.

"How long have you worked as an intelligence agent, Damian? "

"And, a point for you, my American friend." Damian finished his beer as the waitress returned to claim his empty bottle and my glass, replacing them both.

"I went to the arts academy, to be a dancer."

"A dancer," I asked.

He still had a tight figure, maybe five and half feet tall, with slight but strong shoulders. Age had had its way with his mid-section, but not much. I could easily envision him, 20 or 25 years ago, a member of a dance troupe.

"Yes; I studied many years. After graduating, I traveled with the Cuban National ballet…we went everywhere, London, Beijing; los Americas, también, Buenos Aries, Caracas, Mexico…New York."

"Moscow," I teased.

"Si; Moscú," he sipped his beer. "Many times."

"You were that good?"

"No, I wasn't…I did not travel as a dancer. I traveled with the dancers. You know…"

"You… made sure everyone always made it back to the hotel alright….that kind of thing, huh, Damian?"

"Yes, you could put it that way…That is a good way to put it. Sometimes, people need help when they travel." He was, again, staring out to sea, northward.

"And, you've been helping travelers ever since?"

"Más o menos. During the Special Period I helped

the government acquire construction supplies… then, later, assisted some of the athletes that came for the games."

"You paid off Venezuelan bureaucrats, then kept Pan American athletes from getting… lost"

Damian shot a look through my eyes into the back of my head, then softened. "Drink your mojito, Patrick.

"There is nothing wrong with making sure people don't get lost, Patrick. Was it two years? That first time, then another year and a half, later?"

"It was 16 months." I swallowed sweet, aged, mint-garnished, refreshment. "The second time."

"I am glad to know you have left Texas, and it is nice that you are here, in Cuba. I wanted to meet you when I saw your visa application for this poetry festival. We have good internet at my agency, you know…How is it? Broadband?"

"Well," I smiled back, relaxed and free, "I am glad that the Special Period is in the past…and, that there is broadband internet at your agency."

Damian looked up, past me and over my shoulder. Our delegation's driver was signaling from the hotel hallway, outside the bar.

"And, now, I work for a tour agency, helping visitors enjoy themselves on our island." Damian flashed his best tourist bureau smile.

"But, it's not the same, is it" I asked.

"No, but we are Cubans, we adapt…You know, this place where we sit…It was a gambling casino, before the Revolution. The place was full, every night, with American gangsters."

"And Cuban dancers," I teased, "Sometimes, the more things change…"

"The more they do not change, huh, Patrick? Finish your drink, I will round up the others, it is time to leave for our dinner. Cinco minutos, okay?" He rose and placed a manicured hand on my shoulder, with just enough pressure to communicate something beyond fraternity. "And then, maybe after, I can join you for a nightcap, at your pensión…to continue this?"

"Maybe, Esteb…Damien. Me gustaria eso…" I lifted the tall, thin, glass again.

"This is not Mexico, my friend," he smiled and left as two women speaking to each other in loud, excited, giggly, Russian entered from the hotel lobby.

300 Words

In those days, if I happened to learn or discover anything new, I always felt like I'd stumbled upon some secret that everyone else already knew but had chosen not to tell me.

She, in comparison, would make as though she now possessed knowledge or experience far beyond those of her contemporaries. Each lesson learned was an epic victory, won at great peril, far beyond the abilities of mere others.

I embraced and appreciated her omniscience. I loved her for it.

There was something about the way it made me feel inside when she'd pull into the Starbucks drive through and order flat white lattes, and pay for them, never asking if I wanted anything or not. The way she established, right from our first date, that the sexual politics between us would be firmly fixed. I would be her support system, and she, in return, would deconstruct the parts of me that held me back, creatively, socially, erotically. She'd tear me down, if I trusted in how she'd build me back up. It worked.

She freed me from that 100 year old, wood framed, rental in that cow-hide town, and finally got me back out west, and writing.

She said that we'd be together until she needed more, and when she did, and more meant "more than me", she'd move on.

We were happy together for just under five years, and then, after midnight on a Saturday, at the Las Vegas airport, with all the flights grounded in a rainstorm, she did.

She decided to move on.

I got married in that city once, another lifetime ago,

so, maybe it was just the completion of Karma. Maybe it was Wayne Newton feedback through terminal speakers. Maybe I fucked up somewhere. Maybe it was just time.

For her.
For me.

PW Covington is a bisexual cis male living in Northern New Mexico, two blocks off Historic Route 66. He travels widely to share his writing and support a range of progressive causes and kick-ass people. He is a 100% service connected disabled veteran of the United States Air Force and convicted felon.
He may be found on Instagram @BeatPW
www.pwcovington.com

OTHER BOOKS by PW COVINGTON

Like the Prayers of an Infidel; One American Airman's Experience (poetry)

I Did Not Go Looking for This (poetry)

Dear Elsa; Letters from a Texas Prison (a novel)

Sacred Wounds (poetry) SLOUGH PRESS

The Motor Hotels of Central Avenue (poetry)

Notas de la Habana (poetry/travel)

ALSO FROM HERCULES PUBLISHING

BEING BEAT

Chuck Taylor, Jr. is a legend in the Southwest literary underground and has been a mentor to a diverse spectrum of writers, in his region and beyond, for decades. Educator, prophet, father, traveler, lover, poet, and publisher; the founder of the legendary Indie publishing house, Slough Press, his latest collection of poetry is an honest and direct look back at his work and life, delivered with a mirthful and, at times, rebellious, candor.

ISBN-13: 978-1721850556

31210946R00086

Made in the USA
Middletown, DE
29 December 2018